THE SHORT STORIES OF A Dungeon Master

BRYCE WARD

The Short Stories of A Dungeon Master by Bryce Ward

Published by Bryce Ward

Brycewards.com

Copyright © 2022 Bryce Ward

Illustrations by Ashvejlou Arts

Book Design by Susan Gerber

Edited by Hannah Skaggs

ISBN: 979-8-9858235-0-9 (print)

First Edition

*To my friends for introducing me to the wonderful world
of Dungeons & Dragons and for inspiring the stories within
this book. May the dice be ever in your favor.*

Contents

Contents

A Hero's Beginnings

So, you want to know my story—where I come from, what I have done, and where I plan to go? Then let us start from the beginning. My name is Jifar Firmclaw, and as you can see, I am no human. I am what is known as dragonborn, hatched during the middle of deep winter in my hometown of Noble's Watch. My mother was dragonborn, and her name was Sapphire Firmclaw. She was a great huntress who traveled the mountainside, hunting great beasts and protecting the local towns from monsters. I guess having sliver scales is the perfect way to stay concealed in these snow-filled mountains. But I digress.

My mother was a great huntress; however, skills alone cannot prevent all injuries. She had been tracking a small herd of white deer out in the high peaks and was ambushed by a werewolf. She managed to fight off the beast and even cut off its front paw, taking it as a trophy. However, the creature got a lucky hit and gashed her stomach. My mother was able to patch herself up, but she feared the risk of sickness and sought out the nearest town. For three days, she walked through deep snow and wailing winds until she reached the road outside of Noble's Watch. That was when her fears came to fruition. Her wound had become infected, and after fighting through the winter's wrath, she was found unconscious just under a mile from Noble's Watch. By a stroke of good luck, the town blacksmith, a man named Clavin Whitewood, discovered her. In a few months, he had nursed her back to good health.

After that, the two fell in love and my mother decided it was time to settle down. They were married that summer, and I hatched the following winter. We were happy. However, it didn't last. The werewolf that had ambushed my mother and lost his paw? He returned and brought friends. They wiped out the village. Those who did not turn were slaughtered. My father distracted them as best he could while my mother fled with me in her arms. I remember watching him fight off the werewolves over my mother's shoulder as we ran into the mountains. That was the last we saw of him, but we could never return to find him as the howls were always near. We stayed on the move, and my mother taught me how to survive, how to hunt. After five years of hiding in the mountains, we discovered where those monsters slept, and we became the hunters. Slowly, over the next few years, we hunted them down one by one. Then we cornered the alpha that my mother had first encountered all those years before. Even with a paw missing, he was still a dangerous foe.

My mother fought him alone while I took a position on the cliffside with my bow and helped where I could. She leapt in and out of the monster's reach, each time slashing him with her sword. With every slash of her blade and every puncture from my bow, the werewolf grew weaker and more desperate.

However, the creature was quick to adapt and kept us on our feet. He managed to deliver a blow to my mother. Knocked across the cave, she hit her head hard on the wall, dropping her sword. In an instant, the werewolf was closing in on her. I broke into a mad dash from my spot overlooking the chamber, snatched up my mother's sword, and put myself between her and the beast. The werewolf seemed not to notice me until the last second. However, it was too late for him. He stopped, then looked down in time to see me pushing my mother's blade through his heart. The werewolf was no more.

I rushed over to her, fearing the worst. She was awake, but severely injured. Besides a few gashes, the blow had managed to break her rib cage, and she was bleeding out from the inside. There was nothing I could do. The closest village was a month away, even if the werewolves had not destroyed the town. I felt that I had failed. It was the only time in my life I ever truly wept. I buried my mother at the mouth of the cave with that monster's head on a stake, her final trophy before leaving this world. To this day, you can still find the grave marked on a nearby wall. The inscription reads, "To Sapphire, the greatest huntress and mother a son could ask for. May she rest in peace." As for the werewolf, his skull remains as a warning to those who seek to become monsters: they will be hunted down, and no mercy will be given.

And as for me, I kept my mother's sword, which she had named Sapphire's Flame for its light blue center and silver edges. Now I wander the world, hunting monsters and those who threaten to destroy loving families like my own—for no family should have to bury a loved one as I had to.

Bandit Talk

A LAUGH RANG OUT. "Did you see the look on that dragonborn's face when we jumped his caravan?" Ivan said. "That look of surprise was worth it!"

"He certainly looked pissed once we had him surrounded. Shame we had to leave him alive. I hear dragonborn scales fetch a high price on the market," Cooper replied.

"Course they do, but the boss said to leave him alive! From what I heard, the boss made a deal with someone in the merchant' guild."

Cooper's eyebrows rose. "Really? Who'd he make a deal with?"

"Not sure who exactly." Ivan shook his head. "The boss is cautious with that stuff. It makes for bad business if everyone knows who our informants are."

"Well, that makes sense, I guess, but how do you know it's someone from the guild, Ivan?"

"Ah, good question, Cooper! Well, that dragonborn was a new hotshot member of the guild. I heard he managed to secure some new trade deals with a dwarf clan, the IronBeards. Gold and materials in exchange for their jewelry or something like that. I'm no merchant, Cooper, but remember—money talks."

"Hey, Ivan, if that dragonborn was new to the merchant guild, then how did he get all the stuff to put together that caravan?"

"Now you're asking me some interesting questions. Make sure the boss doesn't hear you asking such things!"

"I won't, Ivan. You can count on me!"

"Good lad! To answer your question, I'm betting he borrowed those goods from the guild in exchange for a share of the profits. Since he doesn't have anything to sell the dwarves and nothing to show to his guild, he will have to work to pay what he owes. Else he'll be skinned, and his hide sold to the highest bidder."

"But Ivan, why would someone from the guild sabotage their investment?"

"Can't say for sure, Cooper. Greed, perhaps? The boss is selling many of the goods back to that informant. Easier to sell raw goods instead of artwork. Fewer questions get asked about them."

"Oy! Ivan! Cooper! I ain't paying you two to gossip now;

get back to work! We gotta get these goods moved before sunrise. Now, move it!"

"Yes, Boss!"

"Right to it, Boss! Ivan and I will get this stuff moved before you can even count your money!"

Captain Goldheart and the Ghost Ship of Atlerdorn

"Two months! Two bloody months at sea, and not even a clue of where that damn thing drifted off to!" Captain Goldheart slammed his fist onto the table, knocking an ink bottle to the floor. "If we don't find that ship soon, we'll have to cut our losses and turn back."

"Captain!" shouted the sailor as he burst into the captain's cabin. "We found it!"

Without a word, Captain Goldheart rushed onto the deck and grabbed a spyglass from his pouch.

"Look there, sir, just through the fog!"

As his eye adjusted to the spyglass, he could see the behemoth stone ship piercing through the fog, drawing ever closer. "There she is, the Ghost Ship of Atlerdorn." Returning the spyglass to his pouch, Captain Goldheart climbed up to the main deck.

"All right, lads!" he shouted, commanding his crew's attention. "Listen up, everyone, and listen well as I'm only going to say this once! After many years of riding these waves and trading what we could to earn an honest living for our families back home, it is time for us to make our fortune! Today we have found the chance of a lifetime to bring home relics of the past! Today we board the Ghost Ship of Atlerdorn!"

Suddenly a shadow fell across the ship as the Ghost Ship left the fog bank, towering above the crew like a mountain.

The captain continued. "Many of you have already heard the rumors of the Ghost Ship. Great treasures lie within that ship, ready to be taken! But with great reward comes risk. I do not know what we will find within that floating fortress. Be it monsters, traps, or spirits of those long dead, we will overcome them! Together we shall claim what is ours and return home as heroes for the ages!"

The crew burst into cheers, hooting and hollering as they prepared the harpoon launchers.

"Fire!" shouted the quartermaster. Each harpoon found its mark as it crashed into the stone hull of the Ghost Ship.

With the lines secured by the crew, Captain Goldheart led the way as they began to climb into the belly of the monstrous vessel. A great fortune and untold dangers awaited them inside the Ghost Ship of Atlerdorn.

The Cult's Mask

INE! FINE! I'll tell you why people call me Relic Breaker, but only if you stop pestering me about it.

I'm only going to tell you this once, so you'd better listen up. This story brings back memories I'd rather not relive.

It started when I was a child. I must have been about four or five years old at the time. My father had taken the family out into the country to fulfill my mother's dream of building a homestead. It was much better than living in the rat-infested city of Raclelum. I mainly helped my mother in the garden while my father hunted in the nearby woods for deer and rabbit. Life was peaceful—that is, until the cult came.

A band of figures arrived on horseback and raided our home. My father was cut down like wheat, and my mother was burned alive. She was trapped within our home as one of the figures set it ablaze with a ball of fire that he produced from his hand. I should have died that day, but instead I was captured by the cult. They threw me into a cage and took me to their hideout, a ruined pyramid buried deep in the forest and hidden by a fog that seemed alive. I could hear ghostly voices, and I saw faces form in the mist.

Yes, this is where it happened. Just give me time, and I'll explain.

Once we arrived at the pyramid, another group of four hooded figures lifted my cage off the horse and took me into the temple. I could hear them chanting in raspy voices, and the chanting grew louder and louder as we went deeper into the temple. We entered a large central chamber with a raised platform in the middle.

On the platform, I saw a figure that I assumed was the cult's leader. He wore a white theater mask. Although I could not see his face, I could tell that he was smiling like a father witnessing his child's birth. He was hunched over, leaning on a wooden staff. My carriers lifted my cage onto the platform, and the leader opened the cage. He beckoned me out and turned me to face the others below the platform. Then he reached into his cloak and pulled out a black mask with dark rubies for its eyes. The chanting grew to a deafening pitch as he placed the mask over my face.

The mask latched onto my face like a leech. I screamed and tried to tear it off, but it felt like my very soul was being pulled from my body. That was when I saw it: the demon that this cult worshipped, a large, misshapen creature similar to a fat man. It seemed to have four arms of different sizes and eyes dotted across its body. It was smiling at me with a wide mouthful of sharp teeth, but then it looked at me in confusion.

And this was when I met the one who changed me, who made me who I am now. Suddenly the demon let out a scream and tried to grab me with its meaty hand, but something stopped it. I looked above me to see another creature of pure shadow lashing out at the cult's grotesque deity. The demon roared as it attempted to strike the shadow with its fists, but the shadow restrained its blows, and its roar turned to screams of pain. The demon's arms began to twist and crumble as the shadow multiplied and slowly crawled over its body. Meanwhile, the nearby cultists screamed in pain as if they were connected to the demon. Their leader tried to stab me with a knife, but before he could even pull out the blade, the shadow impaled him through the heart. The remaining cultists fell to the ground dead as the shadow consumed the demon.

What happened to the mask? I'm getting to that. It simply crumbled to ash. From what I can remember, the shadow guided me out of the temple, and I managed to find a village where I stayed for the next few years. Ever since then, I have always seen the shadow watching and guiding me to hunt down more relics of power like the cult's mask. I don't know what it is or what it wants with me. From what I can tell, it's old, and it's trying to recover its lost power or something else. I did nothing to deserve the name Relic Breaker, but those who have heard about my missions gave it to me.

All right, you got what you wanted. Story time is over, so let me be!

The Exploration of the Dagger Caves

SWEAT DRIPPED FROM LOGNIC'S BROW. The clang of picks echoed through the tunnel as he descended into the cavern below. Suddenly he heard the sound of rock giving away and braced himself. The rope tied to his pack tightened as his brother's hold gave way. After a moment, the rope grew taut as his brother pulled himself back onto the cliffside.

"Thordith!" Lognic called, "are you all right down there?"

"Aye, I'm fine! Damn rock gave way!"

"You gotta watch for those stones, brother! The tricky ones can end this expedition of ours right quick!"

"Yeah, I know! How far are we from the bottom?"

Lognic pulled a torch from his pack and struck the wall to ignite it. Then he dropped the light into the cavern below. The brothers watched as the darkness swallowed the flame.

"Looks like another two hundred feet or so!" said Lognic. "I think I see a cavern entrance!

The two dwarves climbed down to the off-shooting tunnel.

"Thordith, hand me a torch. I'm running fresh out."

"Here you go. At least we're off that damn wall. My arms are killing me."

"I agree. You're lucky I had a good hold on the rocks; otherwise, we'd be another pair of corpses for the next expedition to find."

"Aye. Let's not push our luck then. Shall we?"

With their torches lit, the pair continued deeper into the mountain's depths. Each step of their iron boots boomed throughout the tunnel. Suddenly a click and the tightening of rope broke their rhythmic march.

Lognic screamed as the rope gripped his leg and pulled him into the air.

Thordith unhinged his pickax and readied himself to face the ambushers, but after a moment of watching the shadows dance outside his torchlight, nothing came to challenge him. Nothing. Just silence.

"Thordith! Cut me down!" Thordith followed the trap's simple mechanism and uncovered the securing rope hidden behind a small pile of stones. One slice of his knife, and the rope snapped and dropped Lognic to the ground with a loud thud.

"Are you all right, Lognic?" asked Thordith as he rushed to his brother's side.

"Aye." Lognic regained his footing. "I guess we aren't alone down here. What's with the smirk?"

"You best watch your footing, brother. These stones can be real tricky."

"Oh, shut up. Did you find any clues as to our trap maker?"

"Sadly, no. It was just a simple rope trap. The rope's pretty old . . . Wait a minute." Thordith moved closer to another stack of stones and began removing the rocks, revealing a small tunnel.

Lognic's eyes grew wide. "Looks like our trap maker's shortcut. Shall we?"

"After you, Lognic."

The smell of unclean bodies and rotting meat reached the dwarves long before they entered the goblin's lair. Yet, for a goblin hideout, it was strangely quiet—unnervingly so. The brothers begin to search, making their way cautiously from chamber to chamber. Meals of meat and mushrooms had been left to rot in bowls. Tools and scraps of leather still laid on their stone-carved shelves. The pair said nothing as they investigated the seemingly abandoned lair. They turned into a large chamber with an obelisk standing in its center. The obelisk seemed to descend far into the ground below, and the chamber itself glowed with the shine of gems reflecting the torchlight. Around the obelisk laid the bodies of a dozen goblins, covered in fungus.

"What happened here?" asked Thordith.

As if to answer his question, the bodies began to move.

The shroom-infested corpses awakened and lunged at the dwarves. Lognic struck the first goblin with his pickax, crushing its skull. Thordith readied his crossbow and let loose a volley of blots into the mass of goblins. Several fell to the ground, but they did not die. Lognic ignited a flask of oil and threw it into the horde. The corpses turned to ash and charred bones as the flames consumed them.

"I'm just going to take a wild guess and say don't eat the mushrooms," Thordith muttered.

Lognic agreed. "Let's grab a few gems and return to camp."

"Sounds good to me. I've had enough adventure for the day."

With the infested goblins dealt with, the brothers loaded their packs with gems of various colors and began their long climb back to the surface. Their first expedition ended with success as they were welcomed by their clanmates, who would prepare to climb into the darkness and claim the riches of the Dagger Caves.

WANTED
REWARD 4,000 GO[LD]
CRIMES
-ASSAULT
-THEFT
INDECENT EXPOSU[RE]

An Unlikely Thief

"**H**EY, TOMSON!" Calvin asked, "Are you finished putting up that wanted poster yet?"

"Just got it up. Have you heard anything about this orc? Guy's got a twenty-thousand-gold-piece bounty on his head."

"You haven't heard? That orc broke into the merchant guild's warehouse and made off with a few chests of gold."

Tomson couldn't hide his disbelief. "How'd an orc manage to sneak in? The place was loaded with guards and hounds."

"Aye, it was, lad, but when I talked with one of the boys who were on guard duty during the theft, it wasn't quite what you'd think. The orc arrived a few hours after sundown at the warehouse. He made his way to the side door, which of course was locked. Instead of picking the lock, he placed his ear against the door and punched his arm through! Then he undid the lock and walked in!"

"Oh, bloody hell. Did anyone see him?"

"Just about every guard on duty saw him since he didn't really sneak around but rather walked straight into the place."

"How come no one tried to stop him?"

"They did! However, everyone was scared right out of their minds because whenever the orc came into a room or saw any guards, he'd shout, 'You no see Gork!' Anyone who tried to stop him got whacked on the head and passed out. Those who didn't approach the orc were shaking in their boots, doing their best trying to pretend he wasn't there.

"One of the smarter lads walked out to alert the town watch, but before we arrived, he was gone, along with two chests of gold coins!"

"I swear, Calvin, what is this town coming to?"

Suddenly an orc matching the wanted poster jumped out from behind a crate and whacked Calvin with his wooden club. Before Tomson could react, the orc shouted, "You no see Gork!" He stared at Tomson, turned around, and said, "Must've been the wind." Then he emptied Calvin's pockets and darted into a nearby ally.

Below the Library

Dear Brother Barcona,

I am sorry to be leaving the Sanctuary on such short notice and in an unfavorable manner. However, I fear I must depart due to what has happened. Please do not follow me.

As you know, I was not one to keep many friends since my studies required my attention elsewhere. However, you are one of the few whom I can trust, so I can tell you what happened that night.

During the night of the White-Scaled Moon, I was absorbed in my studies in the older sections of the library, as was my habit, when I heard something. A cold, sickly voice was calling out to me from somewhere in the Labyrinth of the ancient library. Of course, curious as to who could possibly be down there at such an hour, I followed the voice until I came across a trapdoor hidden in the cobbled flooring. I would never have noticed it had I not stubbed my toes on it.

Upon opening the concealed pathway, I was taken aback by a foul stench. Cursing my weak stomach, I descended into the maw of darkness as the wooden stairs creaked under my talons. After what seemed like hours, I reached the bottom and discovered the source of the foul winds I had encountered.

Bodies, so many, were massed together and oozing a strange green liquid. The sight was unsettling, and I lost what little was left in my stomach. However, the voices beckoned me farther, and against my better judgment, I continued around the mass until I reached a pedestal. Upon it rested a light green crystal shaped like a human, a mother who loved her children, bearing a smile on her face. But in her dark eyes hid something darker, secrets of something more sinister than I dare imagine.

I picked up the artifact and the voices turned to whispers, then nothing. It was silent. Then the masses of bodies began to move closer. The thing almost grabbed my leg, but I managed to get by and sprinted up the stairs. The creature moved deceptively fast. I had barely closed the trap door when it slammed into the hatch. With a howl of defeat at losing its prey, it slipped back into its lair to wait for another meal foolish enough to enter as I did.

Soon I found myself walking back to my quarters, and the whispers returned. The voice was calming and loving like a mother, but something was off. She beckoned me to travel to the East.

I fear I may have found a great evil. I need to remain strong and keep Mother away from those who would serve her.

May He Who Endures guide me and provide me strength.

Your sister in faith,
Luna Greystone

Beware the Spider's Maze

SHE WATCHES THE ADVENTURERS from her perch above. Her many eyes dart back and forth to each party member as they make their way slowly through her maze, her hunting grounds. Her fangs salivate in anticipation of the feast to come. The party, unaware of her presence, moves cautiously around each twist and turn, leaving stones behind to track their movements.

This group is no different from those who have come before. Adventurers have told stories of an impassable maze hiding a great treasure within. Many have set out to find their fortune in the labyrinth, and even fewer have returned. Those who managed to escape came out as ghosts of themselves. The maze drove them to madness; they watched their friends fall to the traps and monsters of the dark. Then they returned to town as little more than gibbering madmen, spreading the story of the maze and the fortune it held, along with a warning. Beware the spider's maze, they said. Beware Arhozis, the Silent Stalker.

But Arhozis knows some won't listen to the warnings. Blinded by their greed, they come into her maze. She watches the party become separated, shouting to each other as the walls shift and the maze changes. Arhozis begins her climb into the labyrinth. It is time she begins the hunt.

Beware Trickster's Bog

THE YOUNG ORC SLASHED his way through the thick brush. Every step into the mud seemed to consume more and more of his legs, but he had to keep moving. He had to warn the tribe. If he couldn't reach them, his family, his tribe, his people would be doomed. Another step forward.

He paused. Had the mud moved? No. That couldn't be right. His mind must have been playing tricks on him. He had been traveling for days nonstop. He had consumed the last of his water a couple of days before. The young warrior's throat was dry, and the mud sapped his energy with every step. At the beginning of their journey, there had been seven warriors. Now he was one. He could still hear their voices. They were calling to him from deep within the fog.

Was he indeed the last one? No, that couldn't be. He

could see his brother's shadow waving to him and calling him closer.

"Brother, is that you?" The orc moved toward the shadow. He moved deeper into the mud until he could hardly feel solid ground beneath his feet.

Something swam past his legs.

"Brother!" The warrior cried out at the shadow, but it didn't move. Panicked, the orc tried to flee back onto solid ground, but it was too late. The crocs were upon him. His message would never reach his tribe. Their fate, just like the young orc's, was sealed in blood.

Captain's Report

THE COUNCIL TASKED THE *Ruby Runner* crew and me to hunt down pirates. The ruffians had been attacking merchant vessels traveling the Southern Route and kidnapping citizens along the Southern Coast to be sold into slavery or worse. This band of slavers and thieves sailed the seas in a stolen merchant ship renamed the *Greedy Fist.*

We began our hunt for the *Greedy Fist* and her crew along the Southern Route, and having been forced by ocean storms, we continued searching near the Southern Coast. After two days of traveling around the coast, we spotted large smoke plumes off the starboard bow. Once we closed the distance, we found the charred remains of Borman's Lookout. The seaside hamlet had been sacked and torched. We found only two survivors: a brother and sister had managed to flee into a hidden shelter in the nearby woods.

These children were in shock when we discovered them, but thankfully they were still sane enough to warn us that it had been the *Greedy Fist* crew who had burned their homes. It turned out the ship had arrived days earlier, demanding payment in supplies and coin. However, when the village elder refused, the pirates descended on the hamlet, killing any who stood against them and enslaving the rest. Anything the pirates couldn't take was instead put to the torch. We found the bodies of those they had massacred, displayed as warnings to any who would dare stand against them.

The scene of devastation understandably shook my crew. However, with a few inspiring words, they became emboldened to bring justice to these monsters.

As fortune would have it, the *Greedy Fist* was spotted three days later, heading north toward the open sea. The *Ruby Runner* moved to engage the pirate ship, exchanging cannon fire. My crew managed to disable the *Greedy Fist's* rudder with a well-aimed cannon shot. It was a sitting duck, and we prepared ourselves to board. After what seemed like hours of melee, most of its crew were stuck down or tied up.

We searched the decks of the ship, finding stolen goods and the remaining Borman's Lookout survivors. We reunited the children we had rescued with their mother. Many of the captives looked severely injured.

As my crew entered the captured ship's gunpowder room, a goblin sparked a powder keg, ripping the ship in two. The *Ruby Runner* took a considerable blow to its port side, cracking the hull. Thanks to the quick thinking and actions of Miss Boldheart, the *Ruby Runner* still sails to this day. Sadly we lost five good sailors during the battle. As for the crew of the *Greedy Fist*, they are now sleeping in the deep sea with what remains of their accursed ship.

—Captain Alexander of the *Ruby Runner*

The Grasp
of Darkness

THE PARTY SAT AROUND the campfire, tired from their journey but in good spirits. The four companions had recently put an end to a bandit clan that had been terrorizing travelers and traders alike. They had been on the way home to share the good news when they decided to rest up for the night.

Leaning against his large bear, the dwarf Barboe spoke. "Eh, Cylvin, nice work holding off those orcs back there. Those lads looked like they could break bones as easily as a twig underfoot. That is, if they could even hit you!" He laughed. "You were dancing around their swings and slashing them down one by one!"

"I appreciate your compliment, Barboe. You weren't too bad of a shot yourself. For a dwarf." The elf chuckled as she placed another log on the fire. "Good enough to almost bring the whole cave down on us with one shot."

"Hey, I heard that, Marcus!" The young man looked up from his journal with a grin on his face. "How was I supposed to know the statute was holding up the cave?"

"Well, we're lucky it didn't hit any of us! At least those bandits won't be causing trouble anymore," piped up the half-ling as she stuffed her face with another biscuit.

"That's true, Ashy. Don't let Marcus get to you, Barboe. I'm just happy to be out of that damn cave," said Cylvin.

"Hmph!" Barboe crossed his arms with a sour look.

"Say, Cylvin, you seemed a bit more tense than usual when we were inside the cave. What was that about?" asked Marcus.

Cylvin sighed. "If you must know, being in enclosed spaces like that brings back bad memories."

"Really? What's the tale behind that?" replied Barboe.

"Yeah! Tell us the story!" said Ashy as she hopped on top of Barboe's bear, Ingot.

"Very well," said Cylvin, preparing herself. "I grew up with just my father. My mother had passed away during my birth. From what I heard, my father took her death very hard. He became reclusive and shunned those he had once called friends. For years he kept himself locked away in his study, emerging only to gather ingredients for his experiments and often leaving on trips for weeks on end. I mostly stayed away from him and learned from my tutors. It was hard growing up. My studies progressed slowly since every few months, my tutor would disappear into thin air and a new tutor would have to be found. After one of my father's trips, his behavior became even stranger. I often awoke in the middle of the night to see him watching me from the hallway and looking in from the window.

"One night, I woke up to him standing over me. His eyes were hollow. There was no life, no joy, only darkness. He took hold of me and dragged me out of my bed. I screamed and struck him, but he didn't react to the pain. He dragged me down into his study, where he opened a hidden room I had never seen before. The smell of blood hit my senses. Inside was something I would never forget.

"The walls were smeared in blood. There were dark totems made from my former tutors' bones, and in the center of the chamber sat a gold dish, untouched by the gore around it, that held a black orb. The orb pulsed as my father pulled me closer to it. My hand touched the orb, and it felt as if I was thrown into the void. Only it seemed the void around me was closing in, trying to crush me. I tried to fight it, but it was slowly pulling the air from me, and I began to lose consciousness. However, before I closed my eyes, I felt a gentle warmth. I saw my mother. She was smiling, and the darkness seemed to flee.

"I awakened, back in the chamber, to see the orb cracking as light broke through its core. It burst into a large explosion, knocking me away. My father was not so lucky. He began to age rapidly, then crumbled into a pile of dust and cloth."

"Wow. That is some scary business, that is," remarked Barboe.

"Indeed it was. Now, whenever I find myself in an enclosed space, I feel the void closing in, coming to claim its prize once again. That is why I broke off in the cave, Marcus."

"Thank you for telling us, Cylvin. In fact, this reminds me of a tale . . ."

The Investigation of HollowWood

"As some of you may remember, I work as an investigator."

"Oh, really?" mumbled Barboe.

Marcus raised an eyebrow at Barboe and continued his story while circling the campfire. "I had received a letter requesting my presence in HollowWood from someone calling themselves the Owl. HollowWood is a small logging and mining town just south of the Mandu River. The Owl warned of a growing conspiracy in HollowWood and didn't know who to turn to. Apparently some shady work had been going on. Supplies had been going missing, and anyone looking into the matter had disappeared. The Owl informed me that they feared these conspirators might be onto them, and to the Owl's credit, they were right. The letter had been opened before I saw it. The seal had been broken and carefully resealed. However, the forger had used a different type of wax, which gave away the deception.

"I joined a trade caravan heading to HollowWood the next morning and made my preparations for the journey. The journey itself was uninteresting except for a pair of sleazy goblin merchants, but I digress. Since I was dealing with a cloak-and-dagger situation, I decided a false identity would be to my advantage. Luckily for me, the idea had fallen into my lap while I was eating my dinner: an owl's feather, regrettably along with a few droppings. After overcoming my initial disgust, I put together a small but respectable collection of owl feathers. It was none too soon after I completed the collection that we arrived in HollowWood.

"I made my way toward the local pub. The Copper Mug was a decent establishment, a good place for the working man to rest up after a long day. The owner had a large copper mug hanging above the bar. There were a few other people besides me and the old bartender. Two dwarves were having a drinking contest with two other chaps. One was chugging down his drink while his friend, looking defeated, handed over a coin bag."

"I told you, Ashy!" Barboe burst in. "We dwarves can drink anyone under the table!"

Ashy laughed. "But you haven't seen me drink yet, Barboe! When we get to town, I'll bet you a hundred gold pieces that I can hold it longer than you."

"Oh, you're on!"

"Anyway," Marcus said pointedly, "as I was saying, there was a tough-looking half-orc at the end of the bar, having a drink, when I approached the barkeeper. I requested a room and explained that I was a collector looking for some owl feathers. The half-orc raised an eyebrow at me when I mentioned owls. He got up and left once I finished my conversation with the barkeep.

"I headed up to my room for the night and had started getting settled in when I heard tapping on my window. I opened it cautiously with my dagger in my open hand. Outside, in the night, I saw a cloaked woman wearing a mask made of owl feathers.

"Before I could speak, she covered my mouth. She said, 'Shhhh, don't speak. Your room is being watched. Tomorrow morning, go behind the large gray barn house and look for the lone haystack. I have a safehouse under there. I will tell you more then.' And just like a gust of wind, she was gone.

"The next morning I snuck out of my room bright and early. A young man was passed out on the stairway. To someone on the outside, it looked like the lad had too much to drink; however, on closer inspection of his drink, I noticed a few gilder berries. Seemed like my owl friend had taken precautions to avoid detection, and I did well to do the same. I made my way to the barn house she had described, sticking to the alleyways and away from any unwanted attention.

"It took me a moment to dig through the hay and find the hatch. Inside was an old wine cellar converted into a hideout.

Besides a few bottles, the rack was filled with rolls of parchment. I reached out for one when someone spoke from behind me.

"'I wouldn't touch those if I were you,' she said. I turned to see the young woman from the night before, the Owl. She told me it had taken her a few days to decipher all those letters. Lex was her name; she didn't give me her last name. It turned out Lex was a hunter, risking her life in the wilds to feed her family. Her husband worked as a foreman for the lumber mill in HollowWood. Life was going well for them. Food was on the table and there was spare coin to put their son through school. That was, until the White Hand started taking control.

"It started small. Supplies from the mill and mines were going missing. Then people started going missing. Lex had returned from a hunting trip to find her family gone. Her home had been broken into and a White Hand left on the door as a warning. She went to the guards, but no one was willing to go after the White Hand. They were too scared or were already in the gang's pocket. Lex had taken matters into her own hands and gone into hiding.

"After a week she had tracked down members of the White Hand and learned where they were keeping her family, along with the other townsfolk they had taken. Apparently the White Hand had taken over an abandoned fort in the northern mountains and were keeping prisoners there. That was when she sent the letter to me, requesting aid. She needed help getting into that fort and freeing her people. Seeing as she could not trust anyone in the village, I was her best bet.

"After a two-day trek into the mountains, we reached a cliffside overlooking the fort. The fort was an ancient dwarven stronghold. Strangely enough, we did not see any guards on the walls. Wanting to avoid a possible ambush, we managed to sneak into the fort through a hidden passage-way and into what seemed to be a throne room. Lucky for us, no one seemed to be around. As we made our way deeper into the fort, I was able to make out strange sounds, like the howling of wolves. Lex had found clues that her family had been there, and it seemed they had been moved recently.

"Following the odd bits of nuts and cloth, we found our-selves in a large chamber recently excavated. A smooth, black stone obelisk rose from the ground straight into the cave ceil-ing. Around the obelisk were a series of humanoid statues made of the same stone. Lex cried out when we got closer. The statues were her people, and her family was among them.

"However, she didn't have long to grieve because a lone howl echoed through the chamber. Then, slowly, a creature I could only describe as a wolf walked out from inside the obelisk. It was not like any wolf I had ever seen before. It had snow-white fur and walked like a man. It stared at us with pure black eyes. I ran from that place as fast as I could. Screams rang in my ears throughout my entire run back to HollowWood. That was the last time I saw Lex, and I still see that beast in my dreams, watching and waiting with those cold, dark eyes."

"Sounds like we all have something that haunts us," said Cylvin.

"I agree. Even your good companion Barboe has such a tale. Now listen here, my friends."

The Laughing Curse

"Now gather around, my friends, and let me tell you the tale of when Ingot and I faced a true horror. A horror so horrible, it still haunts me in my rest."

"Are you sure, Barboe? Some of the tales you've told have been a bit far-fetched," said Ashy, chewing on another honey biscuit atop Ingot and passing one to the bear. Ingot licked up the treat as Barboe continued.

"Don't you worry about this one. I'm not stretching this story—much. Anyway, many years ago, this little adventure took place when Ingot was a young cub and I was still working as a trailblazer. My cousins hired me to assist with an expedition to establish a new mine in the Bactoul Jungles. They had found a large deposit of iron with signs of gold under the toxic jungle. My job was to map a route for future caravans from the mine to a little riverside village called Valkdorn.

"After a night spent drinking with my cousins in Valkdorn, I began my trek to the dig site. I made good progress through the overgrowth, cutting my way through with Ingot tied up in a bundle on my back so he wouldn't wander off and end up as some beast's dinner. I had to be very careful out there. Just about everything in the Bactoul Jungles was poisonous and could quickly kill the careless.

"This reminds me of when I was about two days from arriving at the mine. I came across a clearing with small bushes of ripe-looking berries spread out a good five to six feet from each other. I was about to move closer and grab a few berries when I heard rustling from the tree line. I ducked behind a nearby log just as a large boar came into the clearing. That boar was a beast. It looked just as tall as a human with thick, gray tusks. The oversized pig sniffed the air before approaching a bush. The moment that boar touched a berry, the ground sprang to life and snapped up the beast! Damn thing scared the life out of me! It gives me shivers just thinking I had been about to meet the same fate. I made sure to give this clearing a wide berth after seeing that. I can't imagine some poor, hungry traveler coming across those plants and meeting a gruesome end like that boar.

"But meat-eating plants aren't the focus of my tale. No, my friends, what still brings me nightmares to this day is what I saw in the mine. Shortly after my arrival, a few of my kin ran out of the cave, exclaiming that they had found something. The three miners led me and the mine's overseer Braxton into the cave. We discovered the entrance to what we thought was an ancient crypt. Inside the chamber were two giant statues of snakes coiled beside a metal door. Their ruby eyes seemed to be watching us as we examined the room. One of the miners found a sarcophagus opposite the statues. With a few strong heaves, we threw off the lip to reveal the body of a creature I had never seen before. The corpse seemed to have the upper parts of a man and the lower parts of a snake. We picked through the bones and naturally took a few pieces of jewelry. Mainly a few rings, a ceremonial dagger, and a necklace.

"While Braxton and I were examining the body, one of the miners got the door unlocked, cursing under his breath about breaking a couple of lock picks. The doorway revealed stairs that seemed to descend downward forever, but we continued forward, our footsteps echoing down the staircase.

"Our descent came to an end when we encountered a large, spherical chamber. Vines lined the outer walls, and water runoff collected in small channels that fed into a pool at the center of the room. Braxton stepped into the pool and picked up a sword from under the murky waters. With the sword in his hands, he turned to me. A wicked smile came across his face as he slit his hand with the blade. He began to laugh like a madman as blood filled the pool. The water turned red and mysteriously flowed upward through the channels. That was when the undead began to break through the walls. Half-man, half-snake corpses lunged at the miners, killing them.

"Behind Braxton, I saw the bones of a snake-man rise from the pool. I tried to warn him, but it was too late. The snake bite into his neck, draining him. Braxton's corpse dropped to the ground. His face was frozen in a maddening grin. The creature picked up the sword and began to slither toward me, its body regrowing as it approached. Fear overtook me. I was frozen in place, and my body refused to act.

"However, Ingot's cries snapped me out of it, and I ran out of the crypt. As I raced up the stairs, I could hear that monster laughing. It said, 'Run, little prey! Run! I have your scent! Run!'

"I didn't stop running for three days, until I collapsed outside of Valkdorn. When I came to, I learned that my cousins had sent a rescue party to the miner's camp to find any survivors, only to discover bodies. Their faces were frozen in a maddening simile."

Bewitched
and Watching

"**O**H BOY, BARBOE, that was a good one! Man-eating plants and undead snake-men. I've never seen anything like that before, only heard the rumors," said Marcus, throwing another stick into the campfire.

"They're real all right, lad. Lost a lot of my kin that day," replied Barboe, scratching behind Ingot's ear.

"Well, I'm up for one more story tonight. Got any good tales, Ashy?" asked Cylvin.

"Yeah, I'm curious, Ashy. Why do you wear that blindfold?" added Marcus.

"Good question Marcus!" Ashy jumped off of Ingot and climbed onto the nearby log. "Well, listen here, my good friends, and I'll tell the tale of why I wear this blindfold. As you may already know, I wasn't born as a normal halfling." Ashy raised her hand, and small balls of light danced gracefully between her fingers. "I got a bit lucky, or unlucky, depending on how you look at it, when I was born. I came into this world with powers beyond what halflings are known for.

"When I was a baby, my parents had a tough time raising me. Other parents didn't have to worry about their child's temper tantrums turning into a fury of fiery explosions just because they couldn't have another cookie.

"Luckily I was a mostly calm child growing up, and my parents helped me find a way to use my talents to help out. For example, I helped keep the oven's fires going and poured out batter for biscuits and bread. I lived a reasonably normal life, in spite of all this, until my sixth birthday.

"My parents made my favorite treat that morning, honey-glazed biscuits with a pinch of cinnamon. Later that night, they took me out past my bedtime for a special surprise. They had gotten our neighbors to make a firework display just for me. It seemed like the whole village was out to celebrate my birthday. My father let me light the fuse, and with a spark from my hands, the entire sky erupted in a variety of colors. The lights became animals dancing across the sky. Ships were sailing through the smoke, followed by flowers growing in their wake. My friends made a firework that caused biscuits to float away as if on the backs of ants. Everyone was cheering and celebrating the display. That was the happiest moment of my life, but then everything went wrong.

"A dark green light exploded from the town square.

People panicked and screamed as another dark green explosion went off, and another and another. Our homes were burning, and all I could hear was screaming as everyone tried to flee or save their loved ones. That was when I heard a cackle piercing through the screams. It was coming from a being that looked like an elder human. She was bent over, leaning on an old wooden staff for support. Her robe covered her features, but she looked fragile. She raised a wrinkled hand, and another bolt of green light shot out. My father dove in front of my mother, but the spell pierced through him. Their bodies dropped to the ground lifeless, as if their very souls had been ripped from them.

"In a rage, I started throwing fireballs at the hag. My aim was true, but she pulled out a hand mirror and somehow my fireballs flew elsewhere around her. Then she ran up and clutched me with inhuman speed. A wicked grin spread across her face as she picked me up. She placed her hand over my eyes, and a green light filled my vision. I fell to the ground, and as quickly as she had appeared, she was gone. I awoke the following day to find my home in ruins, my friends and family dead. There was nothing left for me, so I decided to leave and hunt down that witch.

"Since then, I have been traveling and learning how to control my powers, growing stronger until I can avenge my family."

"Halfling, you had it rough, and on your birthday no less!" said Barboe.

"Yes, but what happened when she placed her hand over your face?" asked Marcus.

Ashy said nothing. She untied her scarlet blindfold and looked at her companions' shocked faces. The dark green scars in her eye sockets revealed no movement as she stared at them.

The hag cackled to herself as she watched the party from her lair. "Soon, my little Ashy. Soon."

Murder in the Ranks

THE PAIN WAS THE FIRST THING I remembered. My throat felt like it was on fire. The air seemed only to feed the fire with every breath. I wanted to scream, but no sound left my mouth. I had begun to rise from the hospital bed when the guard noticed me.

"Whoa there, friend. It's okay. You're in the camp's medical ward. Just lean back and rest. You took a stab wound to your throat yesterday, gave everyone at the watchtower quite a fright. You're lucky the doc was there; otherwise, you'd be dead right now. Speaking of which, I'd better let him know you're awake." The guard's footsteps echoed off the hospital's stone floors as he left to find Doc.

What happened last night? I wondered. I remember I was finishing my patrol of the southern grounds. It must have been about four hours after sundown, and I was heading back to my barracks to catch some sleep.

But I remembered something else. I had heard someone's footsteps, moving quickly, as if they were being followed. Several steps, then stop. Several steps, then stop. Look around and keep moving. Then another pair of boots, heavier, moved quickly in pursuit. That was when the woman had run into me. She'd turned right just as I rounded the corner. Crash! My lantern had become little more than scrap and broken glass on the ground.

"Sorry!" exclaimed the girl, but she had already turned into a side alley before I could stop her.

Why had she been in such a rush at that hour? I remember thinking, wait—is that blood? as I looked down at the crimson pools marking her path into the alley. Something was wrong. I had followed the trail and found her lying in the passage. Over her stood a man in the night watch's uniform, but it didn't fit him.

"Hold it right there!" I remembered yelling. I had grabbed my blade, but before I could free it from its sheath, he was upon me. He had slashed at my throat in one quick motion and made a run for it. I tried to follow him, but then everything went dark. I was on my back. The other guards surrounded me, and the Doc was mending my wound.

I had witnessed a murder and survived, but I couldn't help but wonder: would I be next?

The Beginnings of a Wizard

THERE IS NOT MUCH KNOWN about Wyndham save that as a baby he was found alone in a small canoe. Abandoned and close to death, Wyndham was rescued by a young woman of Feather's Landing, a librarian by the name of Madison Longthorn. Madison raised Wyndham as her own. However, as he aged, it became more apparent that he was a crossbreed of human and elven heritage. Because of this, the other kids always picked on him for being a "filthy knife-ear." Wyndham had few friends in Feather's Landing, but under the guidance of Madison, he soon grew to have a strong love of books. Wyndham spent his days reading and helping Madison run her library.

But as Wyndham grew, he wished to learn more about the world. He took to learning the ways of magic. Trading what coin he had for every tome on the subject. Wyndham studied, and by his seventeenth birthday, he cast his first spell. As he came of age, his desire to learn forced him to wander the world, seeking answers to many of the world's mysteries. As a goodbye gift, Madison gave Wyndham a medallion she had found around his neck on the day she took him in. The medallion bears his name and the crest of a family that is unknown in Feather's Landing. Wyndham quests to uncover his family history and to become a master of magic.

The Empty Prison

A MIDDLE-AGED MAN enters the cell block. The man walks past the empty cells toward the prison's sole occupant, following the sound of sobbing. His face bears the scars of past battles, illuminated by torchlight. The captain reaches the cell and waves the lone guard away. He doesn't need any loose lips spreading rumors as to why the prison keeps losing prisoners. Of course, the nobles in their high towers don't know about that, nor would they care where their undesirables ended up.

The captain fishes out his key ring and unlocks the cell. The young man is in bad shape. Bruises cover his body, and he sits balled up in the corner, sobbing.

"Please let me go. I didn't do anything wrong!"

The captain stays silent.

"Please!" The prisoner turns toward the captain. "I just want to go home."

"Shh, boy, it's all right. Everything is going to be okay," he replies to the prisoner, gripping his shoulder. With his other hand, he pulls from the secret compartment in his jacket a black theatre mask with ruby eyes.

"No! Please, no!" yells the prisoner as he tries to escape the captain's iron grasp, but alas, he is too weak to resist.

"Calm yourself, boy. You're about to join the family. My family." The Captain places the mask on the prisoner's face and stands back.

The prisoner lets out a scream as the mask's ruby eyes glow with dark power. The young man's skin twists and turns a dark purple as if his body has just been burned in a fire. The prisoner slumps to the floor, dead, but then his body begins to twitch and raises him to his feet.

The captain smiles to himself. "Come. It's time you meet your siblings." He leads the shambling corpse through a hidden passageway and into a vast array of catacombs beneath the prison. The clang of pickaxes can be heard ringing through the tunnels. This is where the prisoners have been going. Each wears a black mask with ruby eyes. Their bodies are nothing more than puppets of their masks.

"Soon, the whole world will be united and join the family. But that day will come. As for today, welcome to the family, my son."

The Everlasting Regiment

THE WEEPING CHASM is a pestilent sore upon the land. Its corrupt blood spills upon the land as a red mist known as the Blood Mist. The Blood Mist awakens ravenous hordes of the dead that seek to consume any living being they can lay their decaying hands upon. Necromancers flock to these forsaken grounds to uncover the Chasm's secrets and grow their unholy armies. Many fall to the very dead they seek to dominate, and the few that manage to survive are driven mad by the Blood Mists. These Maddened Necromancers send their leagues of undead to invade the realms of the living and spread the Blood Mist's corruption.

Aleshire has seen many undead hordes crash against its walls, and each one has failed to take the city. Its people are protected not only by the living but also by its undead guardians, who are known as the Everlasting Regiment. Soldiers who have vowed to defend their homeland are resurrected as willing undead—giving up their eternal rest to guard their families against the hordes of ravenous undead that wail against Aleshire's walls.

The Fall of Everhold

ONCE BELIEVED SOLID WALLS and good equipment were all I needed to protect my home. I helped build the walls of Everhold that repelled hordes of invaders. An orc war party, goblin raiders, and even a dragon failed to break through our defenses. Under our stalwart protection, our little town prospered and grew into a mighty city. We even earned the nickname the Unbreakable City. However, I realize now that I was a fool to believe it would last.

It began when the fog rolled in from the east inside the Dead Swamp. At first, we didn't think much of it. Our men on the walls kept out anything trying to sneak in, so we thought ourselves safe. However, we didn't realize the true danger was to come from within until it was too late. Sickness struck my neighbors one by one. The homes I had built, so full of life, are now little more than abandoned husks.

Everyone was afraid. Some grew desperate and blamed their fellow countrymen for bringing this fate upon us. Fights broke out and quickly turned into lynching mobs. I lost my daughter to the sickness, and the crowds took my dear Martha. She was burned at the stake for fear that she was a witch.

Many tried to flee, but it was no use. The sickness was already among them, and they died a few miles outside the city. Soon there were not enough able-bodied people to bury the dead. People dropped corpses in the streets to rot; however, many were left in their homes. The beds that had comforted them in life were now their caskets in death.

That was, until we saw them approach the gate. Those who tried to flee had returned, their bodies twisted into undead horrors that pounded on the gates. Their moans echoed throughout the streets as the dead rose all across the city. I managed to fight my way through them to one of the outer guard towers. However, the sickness has taken hold, and as I look out over my home, my heart saddens. To whoever finds this, turn back. The Unbreakable City has become a city of the dead.

The Fall of Our World

LISTEN WELL, CHILDREN, and I'll tell you a tale of a time long forgotten. Long ago, this world was home to a great civilization. Its people lived in harmony, and together they worshiped the gods through their pursuit of knowledge. However, some chose to pursue knowledge of the forbidden arts. They brought forth ravenous Darkness upon the world that threatened to devour all life. The Darkness spread like a plague, consuming all. Slowly the power of the gods began to weaken until they too were overtaken by the Darkness. All hope seemed lost until a group of powerful wizards cast out the Darkness. But in doing so, they paid the ultimate price.

The world survived, but its people were broken. The wounds left by the Darkness healed with time; however, of the few that survived, one, an angel servant to a forgotten god of knowledge, vowed to prevent the Darkness from ever returning.

She uncovered how the Darkness had broken into our world. She learned how the cults called forth this ancient evil, but when she looked into the void, it looked back. Her mind broke, and soon she fell from grace. Now she continues to uncover the lost knowledge of the past—trading secrets with those who seek to control powerful magic. Often the very knowledge one gained from this fallen angel would drive them mad. Beware the knowledge you seek, for it could spell doom for you and the entire world.

Bull

The Guardian Construct

"AND WHAT DO WE HAVE HERE?" said Bowiy as he examined the strange metal boulder. Its surface was covered in dirt, and rust had taken root on the top layer. Bowiy continued to dig around the rock, the same one he had crashed into with his plow just moments before. He sighed and wiped the sweat off his brow.

"Martha isn't going to be happy about having to purchase a new blade. Hopefully she won't tan my hide for this. Crops haven't been growing as much as I'd like, but it's better than starving, I guess." He threw aside another shovelful of dirt and prepared to keep on digging. Then a glint caught his eye.

"What the—? Is that a hand?" Bowiy cleared away more of the earth, revealing a metal hand. "Well, I'll be. I gotta bring this back to the barn!" He worked for the next few hours, pushing aside the dirt concealing the metal, until before him lay a man made from metal. Surprisingly the construct was still in one piece despite being buried for however long and left to rot. With help from his ox, Bowiy managed to load the metal man into his wagon, and together they set off home. The wagon strained under the construct's weight, but the pair managed to reach the farmhouse just before sundown.

"There you are, Bowiy! What the heck did you bring back this time?!" yelled a young woman on the front porch.

"Howdy, Martha! Grab Rose, and I'll show you!" Bowiy led the wagon toward the barn door. He unloaded the construct with a great push, and a loud thud could be heard as the metal man hit the ground and came to rest on its side.

"Daddy!" A small girl ran into the barn ahead of Martha.

"Ah! There you are!" Bowiy picked up the little girl and hugged her. Roses in shades of dark red and blue were nestled in her long red hair. "How is your rose patch coming along, my little flower?"

"Great!" said Rose. "Look! I got a new color to grow!" She pulled out a dark purple rose with a golden center.

"Wow! That's beautiful! You remembered to keep the seeds?"

"Yup!"

"Good job!" Bowiy planted a light kiss on his daughter's cheek. "Do you want to see what Daddy found today?"

"Yeah!"

"So I was out in the fields, plowing, when bam! I hit a large rock. Only it wasn't a rock. It was a metal man!"

Martha spoke up. "Wait. Did you break the plow again?!"

Bowiy looked sheepish. "Well, I may have broken the blade."

"Damn it, Bowiy! We don't have the coin for a new one!"

"I know, I know."

While Martha berated Bowiy, they failed to notice that Rose was examining the construct. She hummed as she ran her hands along its shoulders. She could just make out B01L carved on its left shoulder. On the back of the construct's head, Rose noticed the outline of a tiny handprint. She tried her hand and found it fit perfectly inside; however, she cried out and pulled her hand away in pain as a sharp shock shot through her.

Martha and Bowiy rushed to her side.

"Rose!" Bowiy picked up his daughter, and tears fell from her cheeks as he held her in his arms.

"By the stars! Look!" cried Martha as she pulled the two away from the construct.

The metal man's eyes began to glow a dark blue, and its fingers twitched as it came to life. The construct rose to its feet, and soil fell in small chunks as it stood. Its action focused on Rose. Carefully, the construct extended a metal hand toward the girl.

Rose reached out to the construct with her right hand,

on which a black mark was visible. The construct examined the minor burn for a moment with its dark blue, glowing eyes, and suddenly they turned a light green. Slowly the construct's rays healed Rose's hand until the burn mark had vanished entirely.

"I don't believe it. How did he do that?" asked Bowiy, his mouth agape in wonder.

"Can't say. Magic, perhaps?" replied Martha.

Rose piped up. "Daddy! Daddy! Can we keep him?"

"I don't think that's a decision for us to make, Rose. We would have to ask him. I wonder what we should call him."

"Daddy, his name is Bull. See, it says so right there!" Rose pointed to Bull's left shoulder, where B01L was engraved.

"Well then, Bull, welcome to the farm." Bowiy reached out his hand, and Bull shook it.

"I guess we have ourselves a new farmhand, then," remarked Martha. "All right, who wants apple pie?"

The Hallway Wurm

AH, HELLO THERE! So you want to hear of my adventures recording the creatures of this world? No? Well, too bad. Ha! Besides, I can't have you exploring ruins and getting eaten, now can I?

Let us begin, my friend. Have you ever heard of mimics? Sneaky little buggers they are. They mainly take the form of chests so as to lure in unwitting adventurers. But did you know that there exist other types of mimics? Indeed! It's not only chest mimics you can find, but also chair mimics, table mimics, and even smarter door mimics that ask for a toll from travelers. But that's not what I want to tell you about—oh, no.

During my explorations, I came across a fascinating new type of mimic I call the Hallway Wurm. It's a long, narrow beast that likes to fix itself onto underground structures.

The one I found was over twenty yards long! I'll even bet there are Hallway Wurms twice as big.

The interesting thing about them is that once they fix themselves onto an underground passage, they open their mouths and begin to blend in with the surrounding pathway. Their mouths begin to look like a stone hallway ending with a long, dark staircase downward. Of course they can blend in with different types of terrain, but normally it's the same setup: a hallway that turns a corner or ends in a staircase. I was lucky to notice the mismatched bricks leading into the month of a Hallway Wurm before wandering down into its stomach. So before you go exploring the underground, be sure to avoid any suspicious hallways. In fact, give it a good stabbing just to stay on the safe side! Good hunting, my friend!

Signs of Infestation

IVAN WIPED THE SWEAT OFF his forehead. It had been a busy day on the farm, and his bundles of fresh carrots were proof of his honest day of work. This past season had been perfect for his carrot patch, and Ivan was eager to see how his corn had performed, but that would wait for tomorrow. He reached for a freshly uprooted carrot, then drew his hand back quickly after feeling something small bite into his finger. In his haste, Ivan knocked over the bundle, spilling carrots onto the ground. Sensing that its cover was blown, the spider dashed toward the barn; however, Ivan was faster and smashed the offending arachnid under his boot. He sighed and sucked on his wounded finger.

More spiders had been showing up on the farm this year, and rumors had been spreading of giant spiders attacking small livestock that were left outside their pens. Even cattle were not safe from the spider attacks—swarms would surround the beasts and consume them during the night. Ivan picked up his spilled carrots and put them back into the bundle.

After a warm meal of venison and carrot soup, Ivan retired for the night. He was exhausted from a long day of pulling carrots and milking his two cows. Before long, he awoke to the sounds of barking. His old dog Brutis, who usually slept at the end of his bed, was gone.

Ivan jumped out of bed and grabbed his old war ax off the mantle. Brutis had alerted him to wolves on the farm before, and, fearing for his cattle's safety, he rushed to join the trusty animal on the front porch. In the darkness, Ivan spotted two giant wolf spiders moving slowly toward him and his pet. The first spider lunged toward Brutis, its fangs hungering for fresh meat. Brutis managed to avoid the spider, and Ivan swung his ax into its head, killing it. However, the second spider managed to reach Ivan and bit into his leg. In return, Brutis bit the back of the spider's cephalothorax, forcing the crawler to release Ivan's leg as it screeched in agony. Ivan swung his ax and once again delivered a fatal blow.

"Good boy, Brutis," said Ivan as he scratched behind Brutis's ear.

Brutis's ears perked up toward the tree line, and he let out a growl. Ivan scanned the woods. At first he heard hissing, and then he saw the glowing red eyes of a dozen more giant spiders.

"Brutis! To the barn!" yelled Ivan, and the pair sprinted toward safety. The spiders gave chase. One almost managed to catch Brutis, but Ivan pushed the barn door closed, and the spider smashed into it with a loud thud. However, the pair were not safe, and they could hear the spider's claws tapping on the wood as they began to climb atop the barn. Soon the swarm found a weak spot in the roof and crashed through, into the barn. Ivan could hear the screams of his livestock as the spiders slaughtered them. He and Brutis retreated to his hidden stockroom.

Unable to bear the noise, he closed the trapdoor. Weapons, armor, and dry food stores lined the walls. Ivan laid on the bed he had installed in case he needed to wait out such an attack. Sweat rolled off his forehead as he drifted off to sleep. Brutis nuzzled Ivan, seeking comfort from the terrifying fate they had just escaped, but Ivan didn't move. The dog lifted his master's arm with his nose, but it dropped to the ground limply. His human wasn't breathing. The spider's poison had done its work, and Ivan had succumbed to his wound. Brutis laid next to his master, waiting for him to rise and scratch his ear, but Ivan was gone.

The Lake's Reflection

W E HAVE AN OLD TRADITION in my village. Upon a child's eighteenth birthday, the youth travels to the upper lake above the village. Then the initiate swims to the lake's bottom and retrieves an item from the lake bed. I have seen people bring up pearls, rocks, fish, and even a boot! It's my village's way of celebrating coming of age and the beginning of one's life. The village elders also bring offerings to the lake to thank it for continuing to nurture the village. I heard stories that a spirit lives in the lake, but I brushed them off as legends when I was a youngling. However, when the time came for me to dive into the lake bed, I saw the truth for myself.

The water was cool despite the summer heat. I swam to the middle of the lake before I began my dive. One could not see very far into the water on the surface, but the water grew clearer as I swam deeper and deeper. I could see the entirety of the lake bed. Fish swam overhead, and plants reached toward the sky. But something caught my eye in the small patch of coral: a cave entrance just big enough for me to squeeze into. I discovered a small underground cavern. I was surprised to find such a thing down there, and it even had enough air to breathe.

Inside the chamber was a small pool with a waterfall leading back into the opening I had come through. When I climbed out of the hole, water from the pool rose and took the shape of a young woman.

She smiled at me and spoke. "Welcome, little one. Come—you must be cold. Please join me." She reached out her arm and helped me as I climbed into the pool, finding a rock to sit upon. The water was warm and felt so welcoming after swimming in the coldness of the lake. Once I was comfortable, she spoke.

"It's been a long time since someone has found my home. The last person who visited me was your great-grandfather. Yes, and I can see that you have his look of determination. He was the one who established your village originally and protected my lake from those who would poison its beauty. It is a shame that humans do not live longer lives; however, I admire their determination to protect their loved ones long after death. As for you, little one, let us see what the world holds for you, shall we? Gaze into the pool, my dear, and we shall see what your heart holds sacred."

I gazed into the pool's depths. The water became as dark as the night sky, and it seemed I was no longer in the cave. I was floating in the vastness of space, with the stars blinking at me from beyond my reach. The spirit was nowhere to be seen. Then I saw myself looking back at myself as a child. I raised my hand, and the reflection raised his hand in reply. I reached out to touch my reflection, and it rippled like a pool of water. Next, I saw my reflection begin to grow. I could hear the voices of my childhood, and my thoughts spoke to me. I listened to my mother and father, my friends and neighbors, and the village elders as they raised the young boy I once was into the man I am today. Many had hidden the pain from their pasts, but I could see through the veils they wore.

My father had lost his brother when they were both young. As they were traveling along a mountain path, the cart fell into the valley below. Father survived, but his brother and the others with them were not so lucky. My mother still bore the scars of her childhood. Her parents had been nothing more than cruel bandits who lived in filth. Yet she escaped them and chose to make a better life for herself. My friends and neighbors had their pains as well.

Mothers, fathers, wives, husbands, brothers, and sisters had been lost to the wars raging in their homelands. Everyone had fled to put the past behind them and start anew, to make a better life for their children. I could not help but wonder why I was the lucky one. I'd never known what it meant to lose a loved one or to be forced from one's home.

I was never burdened with such experiences. I only wish to help my people prosper and live in peace. I may not be a lord or a man of great wealth, but I will do what I can to protect my home. Even if it means giving up my life to protect the ones I love, I must try.

Then the void snapped away, and I was back in the cave. The spirit was looking at me. Her eyes focused on my very being.

"You are just like your great-grandfather. You have a good heart, little one. Do not let anyone sway you from what you believe is right. For your choices may heal this broken land and bring its people together to face the future as one. Heroes are what this world needs, but heroes alone can't hold it together. I believe the world has greater plans for you beyond your village. I know not what you will face, but I know you will never face it alone." The spirit handed me a silver medallion with a strange symbol carved into it. "Good-bye, little one."

Just then, I awoke on the lake bed and made a mad dash to the surface. Once I had caught my breath, I made my way back to dry land. The morning's light had already turned to night, and the whole village was surprised to see me alive. I still think about what I saw and what the spirit showed me. I hope that my future is for me to decide and that I will provide a good life for my people.

Last Stop INN

Last Stop Inn

"ARE WE THERE YET?"

"No, Ruby, we still have about three more days of walking before we reach Castle Runeton."

"Remind me again why we didn't buy a horse back in Carver's Cove?"

Otuo gave her the side-eye. "Because we had to pay off the guards after you knocked out three guys you scammed out of five gold pieces."

"They started it! Besides, that fat one was asking for it."

"Well, walking certainty beats sitting in jail," replied Otuo with a smile. "Anyway, let's keep moving. It looks like a storm is starting to move in." He watched as the distant storm crackled with madding thunder, slowly moving down the valley with cruel intent.

"Aw man, not another storm! I don't want to sit out in the rain again, Otuo."

"Yeah, you have a point, sis. My robes are still drying from that last storm a few days ago."

"Look, Otuo! An inn!" Ruby pointed past her brother to a modest two-story building just a short jaunt off the main trail. Light pierced through the window shutters, and a wooden sign hung above the main entrance. The sign's hinges creaked in the afternoon breeze. It read: The Last Stop Inn.

Otuo looked suspicious. "What's an inn doing all the way out here?"

"Who cares, Otuo? Let's get down there before that storm arrives."

"All right, fine, Ruby. Let's go."

The siblings raced down the hillside toward the inn. Cutting their way through the mountainside brush, the pair arrive at the inn just as the first sheet of rain began to fall. The smell of fresh beard greeted them as they opened the door. A trio of dwarves was playing dice at a table on the left side of the inn. Two of them burst into laughter as the dice landed, and the third moaned over his lost bet. With a whistle, a young woman came out of the kitchen, holding another round of drinks. The losing dwarf passed her several coins. It seemed he'd had a fit of bad luck that night.

A dragonborn stood behind the bar, cleaning a tankard. His copper scales sparkled in the candlelight, and his sapphire-blue eyes focused on the siblings as the door closed behind them. "Ah! Welcome travelers! Come in, come in! My name is Hecker, and welcome to the Last Stop Inn! What can I do for you?"

"Just some warm food and a comfortable bed, Hecker!" replied Ruby cheerfully.

"Sure thing, little lady." The dragonborn turned and poked his head into the kitchen. "Rufus! Get me two fresh loaves of bread and two bowls of stew! Heather! Grab me the key to number four and bring the food up to the room. We have guests tonight!"

Turning back to his guests, Hecker asked, "So what brings you two this far out from the city?"

"We're on our way to Castle Runeton. We heard the fort commander is looking for people to recover artifacts from some of the nearby ruins," Otuo answered.

"Well, you're on the right path so far. Castle Runeton is about two days east of here. Should be easy going for you two now that you're out of the mountains."

"I'm surprised there's even an inn out here. It's got to be hard getting supplies so far out from any of the towns."

"You're very right, little lady. I chose to set up my inn here since it's the last stop for many travelers going west into the mountains, and for those like yourselves, coming from the west, it's your last stop before heading back into civilization. Hence the name. As for supplies, a fair number of traders come through and unload extra goods here. Helps keep me in business!"

"Well, I do appreciate that you chose to set up here. Having to sleep in the rain is not a fun experience," responded Otuo.

"Indeed, I have had to send a few rescue parties in the

past because of these storms. It looks like you two arrived just in time! Now then, here's the key to your room for the night. Heather will bring you food in just a bit. Get some rest, and I'll see you in the morning. The storm should have blown through by then." And with that, the siblings retired to their room.

Heather delivered fresh loaves of bread and two bowls of hearty stew as Hecker had promised. Ruby and Otuo slept through the night without a care for what seemed like the first time since they had begun their travels.

Dawn broke through the window, gently waking the siblings to a new day. However, as the pair awakened, they were shocked to see that the room had changed during the night. What was once a welcoming and well-kept bedroom now appeared as a run-down ruin. Black mold had taken root and was eating away at the once-mighty white oak walls. The beds themselves were rotting, and there were large holes in the sheets. The night before, they had been freshly cleaned silk sheets with a faint smell of Winter's Rosemary.

"I think I'm going to be sick," said Ruby, holding one hand over her mouth and pointing toward the remains of their dinner.

Otuo could feel his gut tie itself into knots when he saw the rotten remains of the stew and bread. "Come on, Ruby, let's get out of here."

The pair gathered their belongings and made their way downstairs—their footsteps causing the decaying wood to creak with every step.

Ruby gasped when they entered the main room. Tables were broken or thrown about. The bar had been smashed in two. A large hole was all that was left of the door leading into the kitchen.

Otuo heard a cracking sound when he stepped off the stairs. Looking down, he saw the white remains of the dwarven patrons from the night before. Their skulls had been crushed with great strength and thrown down at the foot of the stairs. Above the bar, the inn's dragonborn bartender, Hecker, was pinned to the wall with several daggers. Only his skeleton remained.

Ruby searched a nearby closet for any clues while Otuo surveyed the kitchen and found it in complete disarray. Pots and pans lay scattered across the floor with signs of rust, as if whatever happened here happened many years before Ruby and Otuo arrived. Otuo found the halfling chef, Rufus. His remains were tied above a cooking fire, and his bones looked to have been gnawed upon. As for the waitress, Ruby found Heather's skeleton hiding in the closet. Heather's arms were still holding her legs like a scared child. Unsure what to make of their situation, Otuo and Ruby left the inn. Since then, their dreams have been haunted by what they saw at the Last Stop Inn, and they always will be.

The Model Ship

SOMBRA WALKED CONFIDENTLY into the ship's cramped cafeteria and approached his champions. Shenia sat across from Doradar. Her hands were darting around a tankard, welding pieces of metal to it with the touch of her finger. Doradar watched closely, curious as to what the Fire Genasi was creating.

Careful to put out any rogue sparks that could easily consume the ship if left unchecked, Sombra stood next to the pair and spoke. "What are you doing, Shenia?"

She did not reply, absorbed in her work.

"I think she is putting legs on that tankard," Doradar said. "Told me earlier that she didn't want to get up to grab a drink."

"Sounds like something I would use! Does it work?"

Shenia set the tankard down, and legs similar to a spider

expanded outward. The tankard scurried off the table and climbed onto the bar, waiting to be refilled.

"Amazing, isn't it?" asked Doradar.

"Yes. However, I am not a fan of crawling things that can't even pour a drink. Hence why I use magic to pour and deliver my drinks. Observe." Sombra's hands crackled with a light blue glow of power. A ghostly hand had just begun to form over the table when it suddenly changed to a chaotic collection of red and purple light. Then everything turned white, and the group landed with a splash. With their vision restored, they found themselves in the middle of the ocean. Fog crept around them, obscuring the surrounding water.

"Sombra!" yelled Shenia.

"Well, I seem to have slightly miscalculated."

"Miscalculated?! Do you have any idea where we are? Because I sure do! We are in the middle of the damned ocean!" Pockets of steam popped as the water began to boil around Shenia.

"Whoa, Shenia. Calm down. We have been in a lot worse. I'm sure we can get back to the ship soon. Right, Sombra?" asked Doradar with an eyebrow raised.

"Yeah, sure. Whatever." Shenia's fiery glare turned to curiosity as she spotted a large ship leaving the holdings of the fog. "What the heck is that?"

"Hey! Anyone up there?" yelled Sombra, but the only reply was the creaking of wood from the old ship.

"I guess it's abandoned. Should we check it out, Shenia?"

asked Doradar as he turned toward her just in time to see a figure rise from the depths with a harpoon in hand.

Before Doradar could react, the figure threw the harpoon, piercing Shenia's back. The pain alone caused her to pass out. The water around her turned a crimson red.

"Shenia!" Doradar swam to her side.

"Get her onto the ship! Now!" shouted Sombra as he swam toward the ship.

Doradar grabbed Shenia and, with all his strength, carried her toward the boat. The figure did not sit idle, but dove below the waves with the scent of blood in its nostrils, quickly closing in on its prey. Sombra was the first to reach the ship and boarded with ease. Doradar was not far behind with Shenia on his back. He began to climb, and a sharp pain shot through his leg as jagged teeth ripped into his flesh.

"Ahhhh!"

The creature bit into his leg, attempting to drag him under the water. Sombra acted quickly, using his powers to shoot a ray of frost into the creature's grotesque face. The figure roared in pain as a large chunk of ice formed over its left eye and cheek. Sombra's spell gave Doradar enough time to break free and climb up with Shenia in tow. The figure, sensing its prey was escaping, retreated under the ocean's surface.

Doradar worked quickly to remove the harpoon from Shenia's back.

Sombra took out a small glass bottle with a red liquid

from his satchel and handed it to Doradar. "That's the only healing potion I have, so let's hope it works."

Doradar bit off the bottle's cork and poured the liquid down Shenia's throat. The hole where the harpoon had been closed almost entirely as the potion repaired Shenia's body. She woke with a start and immediately hugged Doradar, holding the Water Genasi close.

Sombra stood and looked toward the ocean. "Guys, you might want to see this."

Doradar and Shenia rose to their feet. "Oh, boy. I hope this is just a nightmare," said Shenia.

In the water sat the figure that had attacked them, glaring with hungry eyes. Then another creature rose above the water, and another, and another. Roughly a hundred of these creatures had risen from the ocean's depths to surround the ship.

"I don't know about you two, but I'm not going swimming anytime soon," remarked Sombra.

"What are they?"

"I don't know, Shenia. In all my life, I have never seen any creatures like them," replied Doradar.

Sombra picked up the harpoon. "They are merfolk, or at least they were."

"What?"

Sombra tossed Doradar the harpoon, blood still dripping from its tip. "That harpoon is made of whalebone, and based on the craftsmanship, I'd bet my money on merfolk.

However, do you see those carvings on it? Those marks are prayers to some dark god in the merfolk tongue. I'm guessing this tribe worships this god, and it has corrupted them in its own twisted image. I have heard some old sailors call them merrow."

"Splendid. More demon-worshipping monsters," replied Shenia.

"So now what? We have no way to get back to town, and I doubt this ship will hold if they try to break in."

"You're right, Doradar. Let's search this ship for supplies and anything else useful," said Sombra.

With their wounds tended to, the party began their search of the seemingly abandoned ship. As they moved through the cabins, the group pieced together the fate of the crew. In what remained of the captain's cabin, Sombra uncovered the captain's log while narrowly rolling out of the way of a portion of the upper deck as it caved in. What could be read of the ledger revealed that the ship had been commissioned to haul sensitive magic items for an unknown buyer. In a recent entry, the captain reported that the black cargo had been affecting the men, causing fits of rambling and madness on the ship.

One sailor on the night watch had disappeared. The lad had been posted in the crow's nest on the night he vanished. All that was found were the words *They watch from below* scratched onto the mast of the crow's nest. The captain believed the black cargo was somehow able to reach out and affect the crew despite the container's bindings. However, it seemed the captain hadn't gotten a chance to investigate further, as the next log entry was nothing more than mad ramblings. They watch from below, it said again and again.

In the belly of the ship, the crew's descent into madness became more apparent. The words *They watch from below* were scratched on every inch of the vessel. Planks creaked with every step and felt as if they could give way at any moment.

"This place gives me the shivers," remarked Shenia.

"I agree," said Doradar. "This ship looks like it should have sank long ago. Yet here it is."

"Don't get too concerned with why this ship is still floating. I'm more concerned about where the bodies are," replied Sombra as he opened the hatch of the cargo hold.

Inside, beyond the scraps that were once the ship's food and cargo, was a metal cell. Behind bars were three wooden chests.

"Doradar, if you would please be a good friend and open the gate," said Sombra.

"With pleasure!" replied Doradar as he ripped the gate off its rusty hinges.

Sombra opened the chest on the right and, to his disappointment, found nothing. The inside of the trunk looked to have once housed an orb. Around its resting place were scorch marks.

Doradar opened the chest on the right. "All right!" he

yelled as he pulled out a bag of coins along with a few bottles filled with a red liquid.

Shenia sighed and opened the middle chest. Inside was a beautifully handcrafted model ship that looked to be the same vessel they were standing in. "My goodness, what craftsmanship," she said, picking it up.

Suddenly the hands of a merrow burst through the floorboards, grabbing Sombra's leg. Shenia and Doradar jumped back in fright. Sombra responded quickly, taking a dagger from his belt and stabbing it into the marrow's arm to release Sombra. The group began to flee from the cargo hold as more hands burst through the boards, attempting to drag the party to their doom. Doradar managed to close the hold's hatch, but the merrow broke through it, chasing after them in a wild frenzy.

The companions took back-to-back positions for their final stand on the deck. The ship continued to sink, and the horde of merrow burst out onto the deck from every direction.

Sombra focused his energy into one final spell only for his power to twist into a beam of red, suddenly turning their vision to white. With a thud and the shouts of a frightened sailor, they found themselves back on their ship, safe from the merrow horde. Shenia trembled as she looked down at the model ship in her hands.

The Path to Redemption

THE YOUNG MAN ENTERED the ruined temple, his right hand covering a wound on his left shoulder. His knightly armor was battered and bloody. His sword was little more than a hilt, and his shield was long gone after saving his life from a ballista bolt.

However, the bolt had left its mark upon his arm. The temple was in ruins. Paintings bore scorch marks, and every statue lay shattered upon the temple floors; only one still stood. The stench of death filled the room. The young knight was the last of his order, and he had failed—failed to protect the order. Failed to protect the people. Failed to protect her. The invaders had shown no mercy.

He fell to his knees before the remaining statue. It was as wounded as the knight before it. The smashed remains of its right arm lay upon the ground alongside the blade it had once held. However, its left arm remained intact, outreached above the knight, holding an iron scale. Even with its wounds of war, the statue still resembled the woman it was modeled after. Her incorruptible beauty made it seem as if the stone were flesh. Though the woman was clothed, there was no doubt about her femininity.

Yet as the man gazed upon her, tears fell from his eyes, for he knew that his love was gone. The invaders had taken her life and, with her, the heart of the people. He had failed to uphold his oath, and for that, he must seek redemption. The order must survive, and the people must be saved from the tyrant's rule. Only in the end could the knight be redeemed and join his love in peace.

The Sailor of Death

HAVE YOU HEARD THE TALE of the *Scarlet Rose*? No? Well, then gather around lads, and I'll tell ye a tale of adventure and evils beyond our understanding.

Many years ago in a small port town of an island nation, far to the Southern reaches of our world, there lived a strongly established elven family called the MuckShoots. This family had founded the little town through hard work at fishing, farming, and mining. Good, honest folks just trying to make a decent living for themselves and their kin.

Well, one day a ship arrived just offshore of the town. It had dark crimson sails. That night, the sky was lit with the roar of cannon fire as the ship began its merciless assault. No one was safe from the slaughter that washed up on that town. Only one person was spared, and that was the youngest lad of the MuckShoot family, Sombra.

The lad was only perhaps five years old, but after he watched his family get butchered, something inside of him snapped. Through his rage, flames danced to the movement of his fingers. This child was furious and turned some of his attackers to ash. However, thanks to the discipline of the pirates' deck wizard, he was quickly subdued and brought aboard their ship.

Those monsters held the boy for years, subjecting him to untold amounts of torture. They tried to break his spirit and control him, but they never truly did. While he was little more than a slave to the pirates under the guidance of the deck wizard, Black Eyes, he gained more control over his powers. As the days became months and the months became years, Sombra grew to love the sea and the ship. The vessel was known as the *Scarlet Rose*, and like poor Sombra, it had been stolen away and pressed into the service of these murderers. Sombra dreamed of the day when he would be free and sail the world as captain of the *Rose*.

Soon he would have his chance at freedom, and it would come in the form of a book. His master Black Eyes was a collector of magical items and knowledge. Sombra found something was calling out to him—a haunted voice, but calming and cool. Sombra was drawn to a plain brown book that looked like it had seen better days. It was written in a language that was foreign to Sombra, yet strangely former.

What was this book, you ask? The young lad had found a book on the forbidden magic of necromancy. After some practice with dead rats and the occasional goblin corpse, Sombra learned how to raise and control the dead. With his newfound powers, Sombra secretly poisoned the slaver crew, then raised those who succumbed and gutted those who managed to resist death. Sombra challenged Black Eyes with his undead swarm and succeed in taking control of his beloved ship.

It is said that he travels the world aboard the *Crimson Rose* with the corpses of those who destroyed his family, hunting murderers and taking them into the ranks of his armada, slowly building a fleet of the dead. So when you're sailing the ocean, beware the *Crimson Rose,* or you too will join its crew in undeath.

The Scarecrow's Curse

"FOUND YOU!" SHOUTED JOHNNY IN TRIUMPH.

Sue abandoned her hiding place underneath the haystack. Bits of straw were stuck to her hair. "How come you keep finding me so easily?" she asked.

"You need to learn to keep quiet. You giggle whenever I'm near. Plus, that's where I was planning on hiding next."

"Aw, man! All right, it's my turn to find you, and I'm not going easy on you!" Sue covered her eyes with her hands and began counting down. "Twenty! Nineteen!"

Johnny turned and ran out of the barn and straight into the cornfield. Even with Sue taking his first hiding spot, he had a good idea for the next one. Running deeper and deeper into the rows and rows of corn, he found it—the old doghouse near the center of the maze.

Father had built it for their guard dog, Bolt, but Bolt had

broken his leash and run off during the night. Their parents had said Bolt must have caught the scent of something and chased it off into the woods at the edge of the farm. Bolt was an excellent guard dog, so their father had set up his doghouse in the center of the cornfield. Johnny had helped his dad build the doghouse, but something was different. A scarecrow was standing across from it. Johnny didn't pay much attention to the straw man as he ducked inside. Sue would find him eventually, but he was sure it would be a couple of hours before then.

Johnny looked out from his hiding spot and froze. The scarecrow stood there, staring at him as if it were watching him. The straw man with its pumpkin head grinned at Johnny as it came alive. Slowly it began to walk closer. Its grin grew into a wicked smile, and its eyes burned with hatred.

Johnny screamed as the scarecrow rushed at him, but it was too late. His family would find what remained of his body, but they would not survive the night. When they arrived at the doghouse, they would meet the same fate— turning the lively homestead into a silent nightmare.

The Ultimate Crime

Adam could hear the soldiers marching long before they reached his home. Their metal boots echoed down the cobblestone street. He let out a sigh. He remembered when the soldiers came and took over the town for their lord. Their army had surrounded the city and demanded half the population as a tribute, or they would put the remaining townsfolk to the sword. Adam cursed the mayor. That damned coward had accepted their terms and betrayed his people, the people he had sworn to protect. Adam would have joined his kin and defended their home as their forefathers had done before.

But alas, Adam could barely walk, let alone wield a sword in combat. His leg had been injured after a horse bucked and threw him over a cliffside. He smiled. At least he had gotten to meet Elizabeth, and they had fallen for each other. Yet it was not to be. She was one of the hundreds that the dragon's army had taken, never to be seen again.

Rumors came back that their people were little more than slaves. They had been sent to build forts and work the land. The new masters' cruelty took many as they worked the people to death. Others were not so lucky. Their lords were all descendants of the Twin-Headed Dragon, a race of dragons that walked like men and stood over the people.

Unfortunately, the lords had inherited their father's cruelty, and many had developed a taste for human flesh. Adam knew why the soldiers had come for him. He told the people about what had become of their kin and the cruelties of the lords. Adam fought the only way he could; with ink and parchment, he told people the truth. And by telling the truth, he had committed the ultimate crime, a crime that was punishable by death, but it was a price that Adam was willing to pay. He would pay it again if by it, his people might be free—free from the Black Dragon's grasp.

The War Council

Lord Bear examined the war map closely. The Black Dragon's army had broken the uneasy truce with Amberfall and was quickly closing in on the city. Lord Bear knew war between his two neighbors could easily spill into his homeland. His advisors had warned him that if he did not choose to support one side or the other soon, he would lose the freedom to choose, and the consequences could spell doom for the realm.

Amberfall was a prosperous trading hub filled with lush farmland. That land could help feed his people in the coming years. However, the future meant very little if they were put to the sword by the Twin Dragon. Lord Bear scowled at the thought of aligning with the Dragon, but he had to put his people first if they were to survive.

"Lord Bear!"

Lord Bear looked up from the maps to see a young man entering the war room. The messenger saluted Lord Bear, who responded in kind.

"Speak."

"My lord, I bring news from Whiterock Keep. An undead host has arisen and taken the fortress. Their leader is an undead knight calling himself the Reclaimer."

"How many people were stationed at Whiterock?"

"Two hundred and sixty-one, my lord. I was the only one to make it out before they were overwhelmed."

Lord Bear slammed his fist on the table and let out a heavy sigh. "Thank you, son, for bringing this dire news to my attention. I will take things from here. You have done your nation a great service. Report to the quartermaster for some warm food and a well-deserved rest."

"Thank you, my lord." The soldier saluted and quickly departed from the chamber, leaving Lord Bear with his advisors.

"My lord, I believe I see an opportunity in these dark times."

Lord Bear turned toward his general and old friend. The old dwarf had gotten him out of more scrapes than he could recount. "Tell me, old friend, what do you see that I do not?"

"With the rise of this death knight comes great risk for our people if we are to put an end to this danger on our own. However, the war amongst our neighbors will undoubtedly lead them to seek your favor, Lord Bear. Perhaps we can push them to remove this threat."

"And in turn, we join the side that emerges victorious?"

The old dwarf nodded. "You are correct, my lord. We would be removing a great danger to our people and would limit the damage this spirit could cause."

Lord Bear considered his words. "We would be able to learn more about our foes and, if possible, find a worthy ally. And what's more, our foes would be weakened if they lost a few of their champions while our allies proved their strength. Very well, old friend. Send ambassadors for their champions. It would seem we have a challenge worthy of heroes."

The Woods
I Used to Run

"I USED TO WALK THIS PATH when I was younger. Before the land was turned to charcoaled stumps and dead soil, that's right. Our home wasn't always like this. I was a youngling when my father built this cabin for my mother. The trees stood tall and proud all around us. There were many dangers more profound in the deep woods. Owlbears and wolves hunt here.

"I remember once I had to fight off an owlbear. That owlbear had been getting too close to the cabin while my father was out hunting. It gave your grandmother an awful fright hearing that screech as the beast tried to break in through the door. Luckily your papa has learned a thing or two about fighting the wild beasts that once lived here.

"However, the forest wasn't only full of dangers; it has its share of beauty as well. Sometimes when I went out exploring and collecting berries, I would hear playful laughter in the woods. Grandfather told me it was the spirits of the forest. Others call them dryads. Grandfather taught me to respect the woods and live in balance with nature. For the dryads were protective of their woods, and any act of aggression would be answered swiftly. But that was not the impression I had when I first met her. She was shy at first, watching from the branches as I explored the land. At the beginning, I only caught glimpses of her as she darted from tree to tree.

"Then, during one of my adventures into the woods collecting berries for my mother's pie, I was ambushed by a group of goblins. I tried to fight them off, but there were too many of them, and that was when she appeared. She stepped out from within the tree, and the woodland creatures rushed to my aid. Squirrels hurled nuts from tree branches, birds pecked heads, and even a great stag crashed into the goblins. The goblins fled in a panic. They were cursing as they retreated toward the canyon.

"Her name was Trixie. She looked almost human, if not for her delicate wooden skin and long leaf-like hair. She was beautiful, to put it simply. Trixie guided me to my home at the forest's edge like a mother protecting her child. From that day on, I visited her whenever I could, and she shared the wonders of the forest with me. We watched nightshade flowers bloom in the darkness of night and played with the young deer during spring. We became friends, and I did everything I could to help her.

"When I came of age, it was time for me to explore the world beyond the woods. As a parting gift, she gave me this bronze locket. Trixie told me the locket would show other spirits that I am a friend of the wilds and guide me in exploring the world. I hugged her and gave her my goodbyes. That was the last time I ever saw her or my family.

"Many years passed before I finally returned home. A home that seems so foreign to me now." The man lifted his head from his wife's belly, her body holding their future. Opening the locket, he pulled a single seed from within it. "The forest is gone, but I am still here, and soon you will come into this world, little one. But before you enter this world, I will nurture the land back—back into the woods I used to explore."

The Writer of Fates

"COME ON! LET'S GO!"

"Wait up, Rupert!"

The two boys ran through the woods, hopping over logs and scaring a rabbit as they leaped past its burrow. Rupert stopped before a large boulder. The roots of a large oak tree held the stone as though digging it out of the ground.

"Wow!" said Rocky, staring at the mighty tree.

"That's not even the best part! Check this out!" replied Rupert as he moved aside a log, revealing a hole under the boulder. "I found this place last week when I was gathering berries. I figured it would make a great hideout. What do you think?"

"Yeah! Let's turn it into our hideout!" Rocky jumped up and down excitedly.

For the next couple of hours, the brothers worked to turn their newfound hideout into a proper fort. Rocky collected sticks and stones to use as pillars, while Rupert dug out more space under the boulder.

"Hey, Rocky! I think I found something."

"What'd you find?"

"It's a small chest! I think we just found someone's treasure!"

"Bring it outside! I want to see it!"

Rupert dug out the box and pushed it toward the entrance. Rocky helped him pull it out, and with a thud, they opened it.

"What is it?" asked Rocky as his brother lifted out an old, worn black notebook.

Rupert opened the notebook and read the first and only entry aloud: "With these drawings, I create life, and with these drawings, I can take away life."

Rocky's forehead wrinkled. "What does that mean?"

"I'm not sure. Let's see if there's anything else in here." Rupert began to flip through the pages, revealing drawing after drawing. Soldiers dressed for war, monsters of terrifying size, and balls of fire filled the pages. Each drawing was more detailed than the last. However, the final drawing was that of a sapling atop a large boulder with flowers growing around it. The rest of the book remained blank, waiting for more illustrations to be made.

"Let me see that pencil, Rocky. I have an idea."

Rocky handed him the pencil and watched over his shoulder with great interest as a crude knight came to life.

"What do you think?" asked Rupert, showing his little brother the drawing.

"I think you need to keep practicing, but it definitely looks like a knight." Suddenly the book began to shake violently and pages flew out in a small tornado. Out of the storm walked a crude human-sized paper knight.

"Wow! How did you do that, Rupert?"

"I—I don't know," said Rupert as he stared at his hands. They were tingling from the casting of his first spell.

"Rupert?! Are you okay?"

Before he could reply, an enraged bear emerged from the dense brush. With a roar, the bear charged the brothers, its teeth bared for an easy meal. The paper knight turned to face the beast, putting itself between the creature and the brothers. The bear slammed into the knight, but the knight held firm. The beast bit into the knight's left arm, but the paper armor was as tough as iron.

The knight returned the attack with a blow from his right fist. The bear recoiled from the impact and released the knight's arm. With his arm free, the paper knight reached out toward Rupert.

"Quick, Rupert, draw him a weapon!" shouted Rocky.

Fearing for their lives, Rupert drew a sword and the book once again shook, sending a wave of paper toward the knight.

Their savior pulled the sword from the paper storm and slashed at the bear. Wounded, the bear cried out in pain and retreated into the deep woods.

Once the threat was gone, the knight then swirled into a storm of paper, returning to the notebook.

"Come on, Rocky, we need to get home."

"That was awesome! We need to go tell Dad about this!"

The imp watched from the brush as the two boys ran back toward their home. The bear she had lured in failed to separate the notebook from the brothers as she planned. No matter—she would have chance to try again. Her master would reward her greatly for bringing him the notebook, and even more significant would her reward be if she brought him a young sorcerer.

There Are
No Villains

"**I** WILL BRING THIS PATHETIC CITY TO ITS KNEES!"

Lord Von sat atop his horse, overlooking Amberfall. His soldiers worked in the heat, preparing the catapults that would break Amberfall's outer walls. The siege had been going well, but there had been some complications. The spies he'd sent into the city a month prior had been caught. Their attempt to turn the local gangs into saboteurs had been discovered when the crew tried to raid a merchant's shop. Idiots, Lord Von thought to himself. Those cutthroats had been ambushed by a group of sellswords and followed back to their hideout, revealing the plot. At least one of his raiding parties had managed to break through and take some pressure off the front. However, his gamble with the Cult of Burden, which had taken control of Amberfall's prison fortress, didn't pay off. Reports suggested the same group that had thwarted his spies had uncovered the cult's presence and destroyed them. Lord Von knew the cult was weak; otherwise, they would have already taken the city. This party's attack only proved it to him.

"My lord!" The messenger broke Lord Von away from his thoughts.

"Speak, whelp," replied the half-dragon.

"News from the southern lines, my lord," said the soldier, handing him a sealed scroll.

Lord Von read the report, and as he read, he could feel the anger burning within. "Soldier is this true?!"

"Yes, my lord. I witnessed the engagement myself."

"I want their heads on pikes for this! One thousand marks to whoever brings me these mercs' heads! And tell the Beastmaster that I have a treat ready for his pets."

"Yes, my lord!" The messenger ran off down the hillside.

It would seem these sell-swords are going to be a problem, Lord Von said to himself. I can't have them breaking my siege engines and freeing my prisoners. That will only give hope to the city, something I cannot afford. This siege needs to be quick; otherwise, we risk the Father's plans. The strong must rule over the weak if we are to survive the coming doom. If a few lives must be lost to save the world, then it is a price I am willing to pay.

Trouble at
Haven's Holdout

AH, WELCOME, EVERYONE! Please come in! Take a seat, and we shall get down to business. So, as you can probably tell, our little community is in a rather tricky situation. Haven's Holdout is located just on the edge of Trickster's Bog, a swampland where everything is trying to deceive you into a death trap. However, for the few of us who call it home, it's a place worth protecting because it's the one place where we can grow Angel's Light, an herb with powerful healing properties and the lifeblood of this backwater town.

With that being said, we have a problem. Something new has emerged from the swamp. This creature is not made of flesh like the crocs that hunt this land. It's a force of nature made from the swamp itself. This thing is made from vines and any plant life it can find, and it seems to enjoy snacking on Angel's Light. Entire fields were wiped out overnight. Our livelihoods are in danger, and our attempts to stop the creature have cost us one of our own. Without our crops, my people will starve, and we will be unable to save those who are in death's grasp. So will you hunt the Shambling Mound and save Heaven's Holdout?

Winter's Embrace

DAY 1: My name is Leo Turner, and today I leave my home to explore this wonderful world. My first challenge will be crossing the Chain Mountains surrounding the Hidden Valley. Not many people leave the valley since the trek is a good month of walking through snowy mountaintops. It doesn't help that monsters live on the peaks. I have even heard stories of white dragons hunting in the Chain Mountains. Oh, how I would love to see a dragon up close, although preferably one that won't try to eat me. I wonder if there are friendly dragons that would let me create a painting of them? Ah, but that is why I must head out into the world! I can't wait around in the valley for inspiration to come to me.

No, I must go and seek it! Now I'll do the final checks of my gear and say my goodbyes to everyone. Then I will set out to find inspiration for my masterpiece.

DAY 3: I have reached the first summit! I can see the whole valley from up here. I can make out the townspeople working in the fields. I'm going to miss the valley, but I can't stop now. The whole world is before me, and I must see what there is to see. The other side of the summit is just as impressive. Mountains as far I can see, snow, and even a few pine trees, but mainly just snow. The view is breathtaking, and I mean that. The air is thinner up here. I'll begin my descent shortly, once I finish my sketches. I want to have something to remind me of my journeys. Who knows, maybe I'll find another town where I can sell my paintings.

DAY 7: I can't believe it! I spotted a white dragon! He flew right over me, but I don't think he saw me. I guess I was lucky since I was already resting under the cover of a large pine tree. What bothered me, though, was that I didn't have any idea he was around. I didn't hear anything besides the wind. I wonder what it would be like to fly across the sky. Probably a lot easier than trekking through the mountains.

Well, I think that's enough excitement for one day. I don't want to end up as lunch, so I'm going to spend the night under the pine. It should help keep the snow off me, and it's relatively warm in here as well. I'll make a quick sketch of that dragon, and then I'll get something to eat.

DAY 10: Damn weather! One moment the sky was clear, and now it's a blizzard! I found a pine tree, but I'm running out of fuel for the fire. Even with the fire, I feel my bones freezing. It's just getting colder. So cold. It's so cold.

DAY 12 (OR 13?): I'm alive! I can't believe it, but here I am, still breathing. As luck would have it, a hunter or fellow traveler must have found me and carried me into this cave. The fire seems to have gotten fed with fresh logs, so my guess is whoever saved me just left some time ago. They left my clothing near the flames to dry.

This hunter must have a pet of some kind as my clothing has bits of white and black fur. It reminds me of the times I was covered in dog hair after Robbie jumped on me back home.

I'm guessing my mysterious rescuer is a hunter since who else would be crazy enough to be living out in the mountains? Plus, when I woke up, I was covered with wrappings smeared in some strange paste. It smells of sap. No, not sap earwax, maybe? Gross.

DAY 14: I have decided to stay in the cave for the time being. The blizzard is still raging outside, and I don't want to risk freezing to death again. At least it's nice and warm in here. My only worry is that I don't have much food left. Maybe a few days at best. I hope this storm passes soon.

The hunter has returned! She certainly wasn't what I was expecting. She appears more like a snow leopard than a human. That explains why there were bits of fur everywhere. I have never seen anything like her kind before.

She did give me quite a fright when I turned around, and she was standing there. I almost had a heart attack. I didn't even hear her enter the cave. Oh, and her name is Luna! Don't want to be rude and forget her name. Good thing I have this journal to keep track of these things. I'll see if I can sketch her as well.

DAY 17: Last night, Luna came back from a hunting trip badly hurt. I waved to her when she stepped inside, but she fell to the ground unconscious, and then I saw the marks. She had deep gashes on her back that looked like claw marks. I spent the whole night tending to her, and I managed to close the wounds and bandage her up.

Thank you, Nicky, for teaching me to sew. The others may have thought it wasn't as fun as hunting, but what you taught me may have just saved a life. I even added that earwax stuff Luna used on me for good measure. I hope it works. She is still breathing, but I'm worried that whatever attacked her might have followed her back to the cave.

The storm is starting to let up. I have made up my mind that once I get our gear packed up, I will take Luna to find help. I can't leave her behind. Otherwise, she could die from her wounds, or worse, that monster might see her. However, the creature might follow us during the trip, but that's a risk I am willing to take. No point waiting around like raccoons in a trap.

DAY 19: I have fashioned a sled to make carrying Luna a bit easier. She is still alive, but her head is warm to the touch. I made her soup and got her to drink some. It didn't help that she was still in a deep sleep. At least I got something warm into her.

Good thing the storm has passed. It will make traveling much safer, although I fear being spotted by that white dragon I saw a few weeks ago or by whatever attacked Luna. I can see the sky now. It's time to go. Stay strong, Luna, and you will make it through this. I will do everything I can. That's a promise.

A Bedtime Story

"MOMMY, TELL ME A STORY, PLEASE! PLEASE!"

"All right, my little Rose. I will tell you a story, and then you must sleep as we have a busy day tomorrow."

"I will! I promise!"

"A long time ago, a small village was founded alongside a great river that connected two mighty kingdoms. Clothes of the finest quality and jewels of great beauty, along with other wondrous treasures, were traded in this village. The village was quickly growing into the wealthiest city in all the land. Craftsmen and merchants gathered from all over to master their crafts and take part in building a new city. Soon they made plans to build a mighty castle fit for a king in this prosperous new polis. Yet, while all their wealth brought greatness to the city's honest people, it also caught the eyes of a tyrant.

In the Eastern Mountains ruled a dragon who hungered for the city's wealth. The dragon sent her armies of orcs and goblins to plunder and steal its treasure. Soon the dragon's army faced the guardians of this great city. Men and women rose to the defense of their families and their homes, but it was not enough. While the city's defenders did what they could to repel the invaders, those who were not killed in the fighting were captured by the orcs and sent back to the mountains as slaves.

Among them was a young woman called Xenia.

Tears filled her eyes as she traveled toward the mountains. She had witnessed the last of her family cut down by bloodthirsty orcs. She was the only daughter of her father, a proud and wealthy merchant. Her mother had passed when she was just a little girl. Her father cared for her and taught her everything he knew so that one day she could take over the family business. While she was simple in her features, her mind was where her beauty lay. She was humble and kind to all people, but quick to anger toward those who acted cruelly to their fellow man. Many had tried to win her heart in hopes of gaining her family's wealth, but none had succeeded except for one, a farmer's son named Charles.

Charles was a charming young man who always looked for ways to help his neighbors. His kindness soon brought him into the employment of Xenia's father, and in time the merchant's daughter fell for the farmer's son. They were to be wed in two months, but now Xenia was being marched into the mountains to become an offering to a cruel tyrant.

Charles was not one to lose hope. He gathered those who had lost their loved ones and led them after the orcs. He and his army fought their way into the heart of the evil kingdom, freeing those they found with help from the elves and dwarfs, who also wished to see an end to the tyrant's reign. Charles faced the dragon, but his blades and arrows stuck her ruby scales to no avail.

When all seemed lost, Xenia managed to escape her bindings and draw the dragon's attention away, giving Charles the moment he needed to plunge his sword through the tyrant's eye, slaying her.

With their lady dead, the orcs and goblins began fighting amongst themselves. Only a few tribes of orcs and goblins remained in the mountains, fighting over the scraps of their once-mighty empire. The humans and their allies returned to their cities to rebuild and heal the wounds of war. As for Charles and Xenia, they returned home as heroes and made a life on an honest-sized farm, where they were wed and had one daughter. They named her Rose.

Xenia tucked in her daughter and watched as her chest rose and fell. She was fast asleep. After kissing Rose on the forehead, Xenia blew out the lantern and crept out of the child's room. It was going to be a big day tomorrow, and she needed all the sleep she could get.

Song of the
False Hydra

"Aha! And we are in!" exclaimed the gnome as the lock on the door clicked open.

"'Bout time! Let's get inside. This town is giving me the creeps," said the dwarf as he pushed the gnome into the small townhouse, slamming the door closed behind him.

"Careful, Beldrick! I don't like it any more than you do, but we still need to be careful. Someone could still be here," said the gnome.

"Quit worrying so much, Thea. The place looks like no one has been here in ages," remarked Beldrick as he brushed a thick layer of dust off the nearby bookshelf. The pair walked carefully through the short hallway into a small dining room. The room could comfortably fit a family of four; however, on the table were only bits of scrap wood and something bonded in leather.

"Hey, look—a journal!" observed Thea as she jumped onto a chair to grab the book off the dinner table.

"What's it say? Perhaps a clue as to what happened here?" asked Beldrick.

Thea began to read aloud. "'I went out to the shop to cover for Nickson today, and I noticed something rather strange. Our neighbor from across the street, Bella, seemed to trip over thin air! She hit the cobblestone rather badly, but she just got up and walked off as if nothing had happened! I will have to tell Pia that when she gets home from the stables today. Also, I keep hearing a weird noise everywhere I go. Good thing I keep my journal on me all the time. Helps me keep track of things. Side note—on the way home, I should pick up some flowers from the market for Pia.'"

"What a kind lad," remarked Beldrick.

Thea rolled her eyes and continued reading aloud. "'Something odd is going on. Pia came home from work today saying something's got all the animals down in the stables spooked. A few horses got loose and sprinted out of town! Pia said it's a wonder that she and the owner have managed to keep the place under wraps with just the two of them. I could have sworn the old man had a crew of five helping him. P.S., that noise I keep hearing is still going on. It sounds like singing. It's faint, but I can barely hear it. I asked Pia about it, but she said I am imagining things.'"

"Any idea as to what could have frightened off the horses?" asked Beldrick.

"No. I have no idea. Let me keep reading," replied Thea. She turned back to the book. "'That damn singing is getting louder, and it's keeping me awake at night! At this rate, I am going to have to plug my ears before going to sleep. Pia is getting concerned. I asked her this morning if she was going to visit Bella today for tea, but she gave me a confused look as if I was going mad. Pia said she didn't know Bella, and when I pointed out that Bella lived right across the street, Pia told me no one has lived in that house for years. She thinks I am losing it, and I fear she may be right, but my gut says something is very wrong. Maybe I am just not getting enough sleep. I plan to plug my ears tonight to see if that helps with the singing I keep hearing.'"

"I wonder what is making that singing. Perhaps its source may have something to do with what happened here? What do you think, Thea?"

"I think you may be right," answered Thea. She turned the page and read the last entry. "'She's gone. Pia is gone. Last night I put those plugs in my ears. As I left the washroom to join Pia in bed, I froze. I saw a large head looking at me from outside the bedroom. Pia got out of bed and went to open the window. I couldn't stop her in time. The beast swallowed her whole. Now she is gone. I dare not leave my home. I can see the monster everywhere. Its heads reach all over town. There are no people outside. Just that creature, and it's looking at me. I fear I may be the last one left, and it knows where I am.'"

"That seems to be the last of it," said Thea, looking up from the book to where her partner had stood only moments before. Blood dropped down onto her forehead. She looked up toward the roof and let out a scream as the hydra's head consumed her whole.